The Good Little Wolf

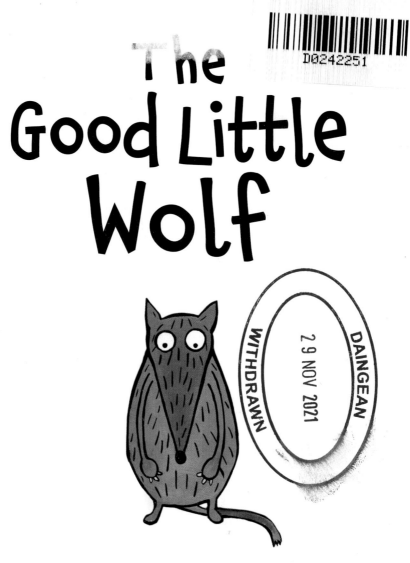

A.H. Benjamin
Illustrated by Sarah Aspinall

BLOOMSBURY EDUCATION
AN IMPRINT OF BLOOMSBURY

LONDON OXFORD NEW YORK NEW DELHI SYDNEY

First published 2010 by
Bloomsbury Education
an imprint of Bloomsbury Publishing Plc
50 Bedford Square, London WC1B 3DP

www.bloomsbury.com

Bloomsbury is a registered trademark of Bloomsbury Publishing Plc

Text copyright © 2010 A.H. Benjamin
Illustrations copyright © 2010 Sarah Aspinall

The rights of A.H. Benjamin and Sarah Aspinall to be identified
as the author and illustrator of this work has been asserted by them
in accordance with the Copyrights, Designs and Patents Act 1988.

ISBN 978-1-4081-2400-0

A CIP catalogue for this book is available from the British Library.

This book is produced using paper that is made from wood grown in
managed, sustainable forests. It is natural, renewable and recyclable.
The logging and manufacturing processes conform to the
environmental regulations of the country of origin.

Printed and bound in India by Replika Press Pvt Ltd

3 5 7 9 10 8 6 4

Chapter One

Once there were two wolves who lived in a cave in a big dark wood. They were called Big Wolf and Little Wolf.

Little Wolf loved hearing stories, so
Big Wolf always told him one at bedtime.
Most of them were about wolves.

"Dad?" asked Little Wolf one night.
"Are all wolves bad?"
"Of course not," replied Big Wolf.
"They are in books," said Little Wolf.

"Those are just stories," said Big Wolf.
"You must not believe what they say.
Now go to sleep, it's late." And he kissed
Little Wolf good night.

It was a long time before Little Wolf fell asleep. But when he did, he had exciting dreams. He was in lots of stories … and he was the hero of each one!

"I'm going to be good today," said Little Wolf, the next morning at breakfast.

"Very well," smiled Big Wolf. "Then off you go."

Little Wolf trotted out of the cave, and into the woods.

"I'll show everyone wolves can be good," he said to himself. "Then someone can write a story about me!"

He liked that idea very much.

Chapter Two

Soon Little Wolf came to a clearing. There he saw an old lady, who was picking mushrooms. She had grey hair and she was wearing glasses.

"She's a grandma," thought Little Wolf. He had seen pictures of grandmas in storybooks.

Then Little Wolf saw something else.
A snake was in the grass behind the old
lady. And she hadn't seen it!

"I must do something," thought Little Wolf. "The grandma is in danger!" With two quick leaps, he pounced on the snake. He grabbed it in his jaws and fiercely shook it about.

The old lady jumped up with surprise.
"You bad wolf," she shrieked. "Leave my
walking stick alone!"

Little Wolf dropped the snake and ran off as fast as he could. He didn't stop running until he came to the edge of the woods.

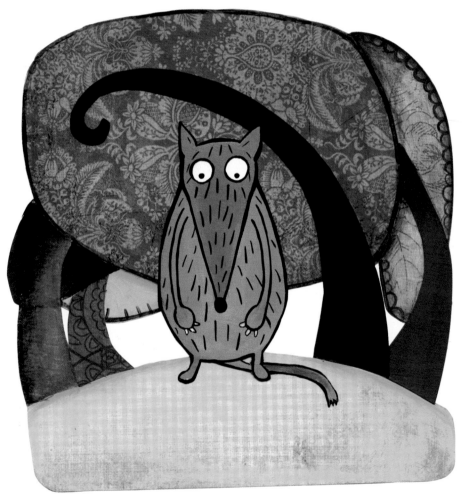

"I tried to be good," he panted. "It's not fair. I'll never be a hero now."

Chapter Three

Not far away, Little Wolf came to a
field. There he saw some white, woolly
creatures. Nearby, a tall, thin man was
sitting on a rock eating his lunch.

"Those are sheep," thought Little Wolf.
"And that's a shepherd." He had seen
pictures of sheep and shepherds in
storybooks.

Just then, one of the sheep moved away from the group.

"What a naughty sheep," thought Little Wolf. "I'll soon sort it out." And he was off in a flash.

A moment later, he was chasing the sheep round and round the field. It was terrified and so were the rest of the flock.

"Baa! Baa!" they bleated, running all over the place.

Little Wolf did not know which sheep to chase. First he chased one …

then he chased another.

The shepherd got to his feet and ran after Little Wolf with his long, crooked staff.

"You bad wolf," he shouted. "Leave my sheep alone!"

Little Wolf stopped chasing the sheep and fled. He didn't stop running until he came to a farm.

"I tried to be good," he panted. "*Twice.* But it's no use. I'll never be a hero now."

Chapter Four

Just then, Little Wolf noticed three pink animals with curly tails. They were shut in a dirty wooden pen.

"Those are pigs," thought Little Wolf. He had seen pictures of pigs in storybooks.

Little Wolf wondered why the pigs lived in such a horrible place. There was a nice cottage with a red door and blue windows not far away. Little Wolf was sure the pigs would prefer to live there instead.

"Maybe they haven't seen it," he thought.
"I'll show them where it is."
Little Wolf jumped inside the pen.

The pigs squealed with fright.
They broke down the fence and trotted
off down the lane.

Little Wolf raced after them, leading the
pigs straight to the pretty cottage.

A young girl with a freckled face stuck her head out of the window. She looked very angry.

"You bad wolf," she screamed. "Leave my pigs alone!"

Little Wolf turned and scampered off.
He did not stop until he was back in the
woods again.

"I tried to be good," he panted. "*Three times*. But it's not working. I'll never be a hero now."

Chapter Five

Little Wolf was sad and fed up. He turned to go back home. He had not gone far when he saw a big, strong man chopping a tree with an axe.

"That's a woodcutter," thought Little
Wolf. He had seen pictures of woodcutters
in storybooks.

"They don't like wolves very much,"
thought Little Wolf. "I'd better keep away
from him!"

He was just about to sneak off, when
something happened.

The tree that the woodcutter was
chopping suddenly started to fall.
He had no time to get out of the way …
and it landed right on top of him.
"Oh, no!" gasped Little Wolf.

Luckily, the woodcutter was not hurt.
But he *was* stuck under the tree.
"Help! Help!" he shouted.

Slowly, Little Wolf came closer.
He wanted to help. But how?
Just then, the woodcutter saw him.
"A wolf," he cried. "That's all I need.
Go away! Leave me alone!"

Little Wolf gave his face a friendly lick.
Just to say, "I'm not going to hurt you."
"Oh," smiled the woodcutter. "Are you a
good wolf? Will you help me?"

He handed Little Wolf his hat. "Here –
take this to the village. When they see it,
they'll know something's wrong. Please,
my friend. Please hurry!"

Little Wolf took the hat in his mouth
and ran off as fast as he could.
"This is my chance to be hero!"
he thought, with excitement.

Chapter Six

Soon Little Wolf reached the village.
The people spotted him at once.
"Wolf! Wolf!" they all shouted.

"That's a bad wolf!" croaked the old lady.
"He tried to steal my walking stick!"

"He chased my sheep!" cried the tall, thin shepherd.

"He frightened my pigs!" squealed the girl with the freckled face.

"Oh, no!" sobbed a boy. "He's got my dad's hat in his mouth. He must have eaten him!"

"Come on," they shouted.
"Let's get the bad little wolf!"
Little Wolf turned on his
heels and the whole village
chased after him …

straight to the spot where the woodcutter
was trapped!

The villagers quickly moved the tree and
the woodcutter got up gratefully.
"Dad," cried the boy, hugging his father.
"You're all right. We thought you had
been eaten by the bad little wolf!"

"He's not a bad little wolf," said the woodcutter. "He's a *good* little wolf." Then he explained what had happened. Everybody was amazed.

Little Wolf just stood there, looking very proud. He was a hero at last!

"Thank you!" said the little boy. "You saved my dad!"

Everyone cheered. "Hooray for the good little wolf!"

"I'm going to write a story about you," promised the woodcutter. "And I'm going to call it *The Good Little Wolf*."

Little Wolf smiled, as if to say, "I like the sound of that!" And happily, he trotted home.